Original Works Ltd.

An   Publication

HAPPY FOREVER- HOME DAY LUNA

Adopted 18·08·2015

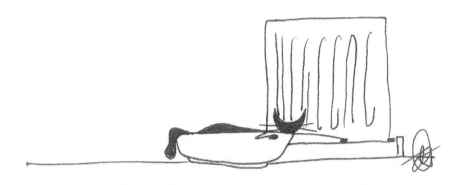

About the Artist

Tina Goode was born and lives on the Isle of Wight. Since early childhood she has loved drawing and cats. In 2015 she and her husband adopted a rescue cat called Luna, and the rest as they say is history...

Printed in Great Britain
by Amazon

83678604R00041